A Royal Wedding Album

By Andrea Posner-Sanchez

Illustrated by the Disney Storybook Art Team

Random House 🏠 New York

ISBN 978-0-7364-3477-5

randomhousekids.com

Printed in the United States of America

10 9 8 7 6 5 4 3 2 1

A royal wedding is a day of celebration!

It's a new beginning full of laughter and love. It's a way to celebrate with family and friends. It's a day of precious memories to come. And it's a good reason to dance, sing, and eat delicious wedding cake!

Turn the page to see how Rapunzel, Belle, Tiana, Cinderella, Aurora, Ariel, Jasmine, and Snow White celebrated their royal weddings.

Falling in Love

There are many ways to meet your one true love. For some, it is love at first sight. For others, it takes a bit longer to fall in love.

Rapunzel had been hidden away for almost eighteen years when Flynn Rider appeared in her tower. What did she do when she saw the handsome stranger? She bopped him on the head with a frying pan! But after an exciting journey to see the floating lights up close, Rapunzel and Flynn fell deeply in love.

Prince Naveen was a frog when Tiana met—and kissed—him! She expected the kiss to make him human again. Instead, Tiana became a frog, too! Hopping around a swamp together made these two realize they loved each other. They had a frog wedding, and their first kiss as husband and wife transformed them back into humans!

Belle didn't like the Beast at all when they first met. He was grumpy and scary and had awful table manners. But Belle soon saw that there was a kind heart beneath all that fur. Once they fell in love, the curse was broken. The Prince and all the enchanted objects in his castle became human again.

Cinderella and her prince fell in love the night they met while dancing at a royal ball. But she had to rush home before even telling him her name. Luckily, Cinderella left one of her glass slippers behind on the palace steps. The Prince and Cinderella found each other, and then they built a new life together!

On Aurora's sixteenth birthday, she met Prince Phillip in the forest and fell in love. The two didn't know that their parents had decided many years before that one day they should marry. Later, when the sleeping beauty was under Maleficent's curse, Prince Phillip's kiss woke her.

Ariel was in love with Prince Eric before they even met! The little mermaid watched the prince on his ship—and bravely rescued him when he fell overboard. After Ariel traded her tail for legs, Eric got to spend time with her on land. He quickly realized he loved her, too.

Princess Jasmine met Aladdin in the marketplace when she was pretending to be a commoner. Later, Aladdin pretended to be a prince to get a chance to marry Jasmine. After some thrilling rides on the Magic Carpet, Jasmine knew she wanted to be with Aladdin forever—even though he wasn't really royal.

Snow White always dreamed of marrying a handsome prince. Luckily, one came back into her life when she needed him most—after she was poisoned by the evil Queen. The Prince's kiss woke Snow White so they could live happily ever after!

Will You Marry Me?

After love comes the marriage proposal—usually with
a declaration of lifelong commitment and devotion.

When Phillip and Aurora were very young, their parents agreed that
they should marry one day. But Phillip knew that Aurora would make
her own decision—he kneeled and asked her to marry him. She said yes!

Flynn proposed to Rapunzel in the same boat they were in when they fell in love.

Snow White was sitting on a horse when the Prince asked if she would spend the rest of her life with him. After she said yes, he tied a pretty flower around her finger, promising to replace it with a real ring later.

Naveen wanted to marry Tiana when they were still frogs. He made her an engagement ring with a bead and some wire and stored it in a walnut shell.

Prince Charming knew that a life with Cinderella would be full of happiness and love. He couldn't wait to propose! Cinderella accepted his proposal—she knew he was the one!

All Dressed Up

Weddings are a special time to get all dressed up! The Disney princesses all chose dresses that reflected their personality.

Belle's dress was covered in roses made of white satin. The roses were special because they are symbols of Belle and the Beast's journey toward friendship and romance.

Tiana's scoop-necked wedding gown was made by her mother, Eudora. Tiana knows the importance of family, and she felt grateful to be shown such a kind and generous act of love.

Aurora's royal dressmakers offered her gowns of many colors and styles. The princess decided to get married in her mother's wedding dress. It fit perfectly!

Rapunzel paired her short-sleeved gown with an extra-long veil. It was a reminder of the beautiful long hair she had, and how far she had come toward living a life of her own choosing.

Ariel's gown was made from fine silk and satin. Carlotta the seamstress made sure the princess would be comfortable walking in it—she was still getting used to her new legs!

Jasmine wanted her wedding gown to look exactly like
the one her mother had worn. The royal seamstress did
her best to make a perfect match.

Cinderella choose a glamorous ball gown for her wedding dress. It was similar to the dress the Fairy Godmother had made for her the night she met the Prince!

Snow White chose a simple wedding gown
with lovely rose-colored accents. The dress
perfectly suited her classic style!

The Guest List

*It wouldn't be a celebration without
friends and family to share the fun!*

Snow White's
Guest List

Dopey

Grumpy

Doc

Sneezy

Bashful

Sleepy

Happy

Jasmine's
Guest List

the Sultan
Rajah
Genie
Abu

Ariel's
Guest List

King Triton
my six sisters
Sebastian
Flounder
Max
Grimsby
Carlotta

Aurora's
Guest List

the King and Queen

King Hubert

Flora

Fauna

Merryweather

Cinderella's
Guest List

Fairy Godmother

the King

the Grand Duke

Gus and Jaq

Bruno

Belle's
Guest List
Maurice

Mrs. Potts

Cogsworth

Lumiere

Chip

Rapunzel's
Guest List
the King and Queen

Pascal

Maximus

the Pub Thugs

Tiana's
Guest List
Eudora

Charlotte

Mr. LaBouff

the King and Queen
of Maldonia

Louis

Special Touches

A wedding ceremony that includes items meaningful
to the bride and groom makes the day even more special.

Jasmine wished her mother could have been a part of her big day.
She found her mother's wedding album and planned her own
wedding to be exactly like her parents'.

Cinderella had the royal jeweler create a new necklace. It combined the pearls that had been worn by the Prince's mother with the heart-shaped stone given to her by her own mother.

Belle read a passage from one of her favorite books at her ceremony. And the Prince presented her with a journal so she could write about their future adventures together.

Tiana carried her father's old spoon in her wedding bouquet. She knew he would have been thrilled to see her marry a man as kind as Naveen. She also wore the tiara the Queen of Maldonia had worn at her own wedding.

The Prince made Snow White's wedding ring himself. He even mined the perfect diamond—with help from the Seven Dwarfs.

Ariel carried her sister Adella's lucky blue starfish. She wore her sister Aquata's favorite seashell hair clip. And her father gave her a brilliant pink pearl that had belonged to her mother.

I Do!

The ceremony makes everything official! The prince
and princess vow to love each other forever.

The Seven Dwarfs walked Snow White down
the aisle as her forest animal friends looked on.

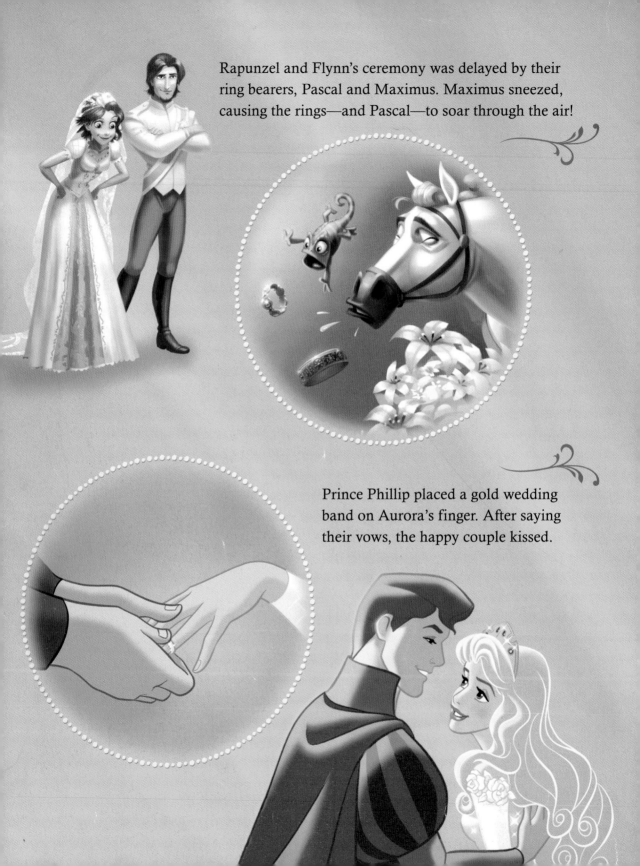

Rapunzel and Flynn's ceremony was delayed by their ring bearers, Pascal and Maximus. Maximus sneezed, causing the rings—and Pascal—to soar through the air!

Prince Phillip placed a gold wedding band on Aurora's finger. After saying their vows, the happy couple kissed.

Tiana missed her father but was happy to have her best friend's father, Mr. LaBouff, walk her down the aisle. Her best friend, Charlotte, was her maid of honor.

Belle walked down a grand staircase on the arm of her father, Maurice. Little Chip was the ring bearer.

Colorful, exotic flowers decorated the aisle at Jasmine and Aladdin's ceremony. Everything was according to the couple's taste!

Ariel and Eric got married on the deck of a ship so that Ariel's merfamily could watch from the water.

The King was proud to walk Cinderella down the aisle.

Time for Cake!

Every wedding needs a delicious cake!

Tiana loves using her cooking skills. She made all the food for her wedding day herself—including the cake.

Rapunzel and Attila the Pub Thug worked together to bake her huge, colorful wedding cake. It was eight layers high!

Mrs. Potts tasted many different flavors to choose the perfect ingredients for Belle's wedding cake. Yum!

Aurora and Phillip fed each other mouthfuls of delicious cake.

Gus tried to get a nibble of tasty wedding cake
as Cinderella and the Prince cut the first slice.

Jasmine asked the royal pastry chef to bake the same cake her parents had enjoyed at their wedding.

Snow White's cake had yummy fresh berries on it.

Chef Louis made two cakes for Ariel and Prince
Eric's wedding—one for the guests aboard the ship
and one for the guests in the water.

Shall We Dance?

It's a tradition for the couple to have the
first dance at their wedding reception.

Belle and the Prince danced outside
as rose petals floated around them.

The good fairies added a touch of magic to Aurora and Phillips's first dance.

Sebastian's undersea orchestra played as Ariel, Eric, and their guests danced.

Rapunzel danced barefoot at her wedding!

Snow White and the Prince danced while the Seven Dwarfs played music.

Happily Ever After

With the celebration over, the prince and princess head off to begin their life together. There's no telling what exciting adventures they'll experience!

Aurora's royal carriage was white and gold—just like the horses that pulled it.

Snow White's animal friends led the way for her wedding carriage.

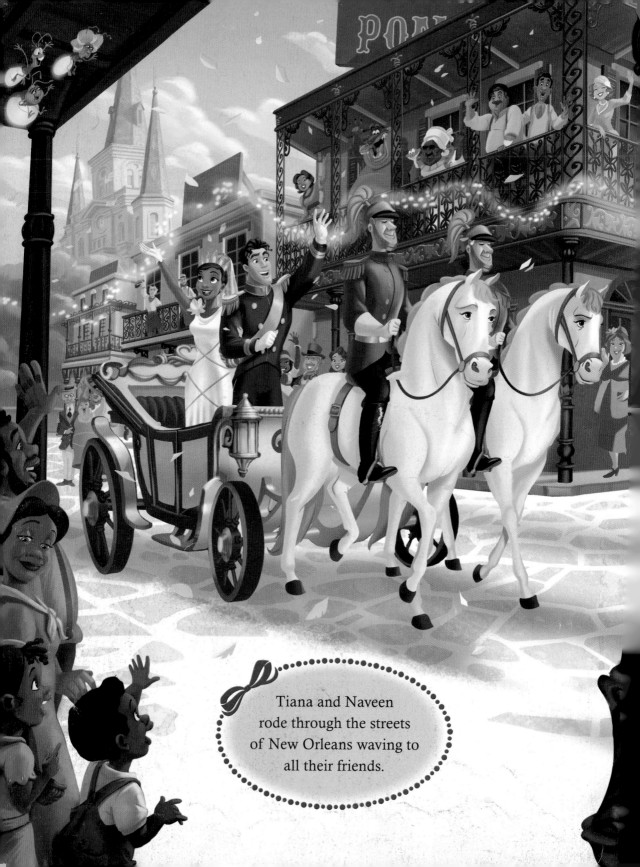

Tiana and Naveen
rode through the streets
of New Orleans waving to
all their friends.

Rapunzel's carriage was decorated by her friends the Pub Thugs.